ANTHON W

A Walk in the Park

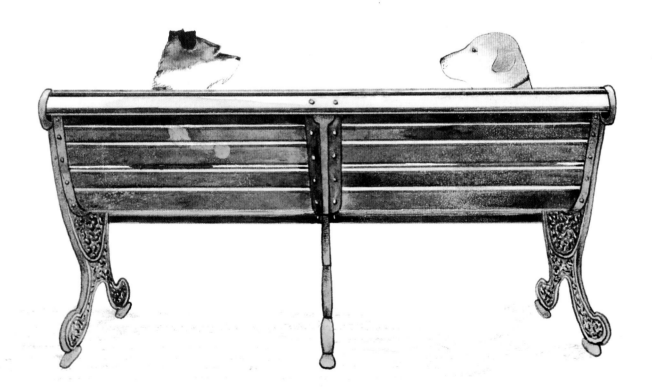

WALKER BOOKS
AND SUBSIDIARIES

LONDON • BOSTON • SYDNEY • AUCKLAND

First published 1977 by Hamish Hamilton Children's Books

This edition published 2013 by Walker Books Ltd
87 Vauxhall Walk, London SE11 5HJ

8 10 9 7

© 1977 Brun Ltd

The right of Anthony Browne to be identified as author/illustrator of this work
has been asserted by him in accordance with the Copyright, Designs and Patents Act 1988

This book has been typeset in New Century Schoolbook

Printed in China

British Library Cataloguing in Publication Data:
a catalogue record for this book is available from the British Library

ISBN 978-1-4063-4164-5

www.walker.co.uk

One morning Mr Smith and his little girl,
Smudge, took their dog, Albert, for a walk.

On that same morning Mrs Smythe and her son,

Charles, were taking their dog, Victoria, for a walk.

Smudge, Mr Smith and Albert
went into the park.

Mrs Smythe, Charles and Victoria
arrived soon afterwards.

Albert was impatient to be let off his lead.

Victoria waited quietly until Mrs Smythe had
detached the lead from her collar.

Both dogs were free.

They chased each other all over the park.

Mr Smith went to sit at one end of a bench
and Smudge sat with him.

Mrs Smythe sat at the other end with Charles.
Smudge and Charles looked at each other.

Albert and Victoria raced along the paths, dodging round trees, leaping over flower beds. First Albert chased Victoria, then Victoria chased Albert, then Albert chased Victoria again, so quickly that sometimes it was difficult to tell them apart.

While the dogs played, Smudge and
Charles edged nearer and nearer
to each other.

Mr Smith and Mrs Smythe looked
the other way.

Smudge went on the swings, swinging
higher and higher, as high as she dared.
Charles was not so sure.

Meanwhile an angry gardener chased
the dogs off the flower beds.

They took off their coats and Smudge swung like a monkey on the climbing frame.

Albert felt too hot, so to cool himself he plunged
into the fountain.

Smudge and Charles climbed a tree.

They all played on the bandstand.

The whole world seemed happy.

But Mr Smith read his newspaper
at one end of the bench and
Mrs Smythe looked the other way.

Charles picked a flower and gave it to Smudge.

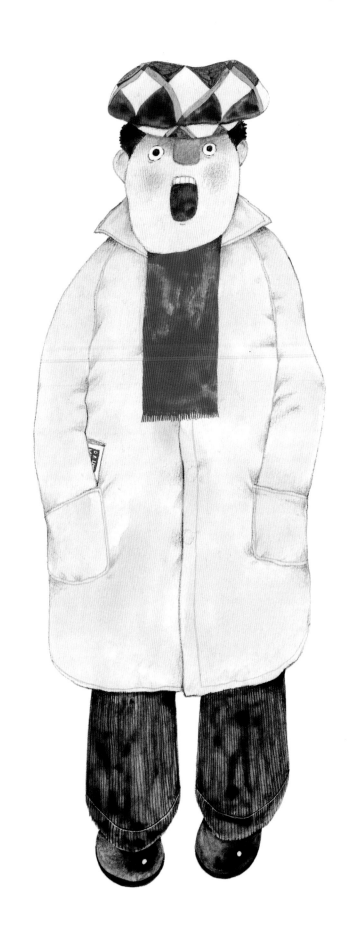

"'Ere Albert, 'ere Smudge," yelled Mr Smith.
"Time for 'ome!"

"Come here Victoria, come along Charles," called Mrs Smythe. "Time for lunch."

Mrs Smythe took Charles and Victoria home.

Mr Smith took home Smudge and Albert.

And Smudge kept the flower.